Sadie
the Saxophone Fairy

by Daisy Meadows

ORCHARD BOOKS

www.rainbowmagic.co.uk

Jack Frost's
Ice Castle

The Park

High Street

The Alley

MUSIC SHOP

Kirsty's House

Fields

Wetherbury Hotel

I'm through with frost, ice and snow.
To the human world I must go!
I'll form a cool, Gobolicious Band.
Magical instruments will lend a hand.

With these instruments I'll go far.
Frosty Jack, a superstar.
I'll steal music's harmony and fun.
Watch out world, I'll be number one!

Contents

The Competition Begins

"We'd better hurry, Kirsty," Rachel Walker said to her best friend, Kirsty Tate, as they jumped out of the car. "The talent competition will be starting soon!"

The girls waved at Mrs Tate, who had just dropped them off, and then they hurried into the New Harmony Shopping Mall.

"Good afternoon, everyone," said a voice over the loudspeaker system as the girls went inside. "The auditions for the National Talent Competition are about to start, so please make your way to the north end of the shopping mall."

Rachel and Kirsty glanced at each other as they wove their way through the crowds.

"There are lots of people here, aren't there?" Kirsty said anxiously. "I hope we get Sadie's Magic Saxophone back before Frosty and his Gobolicious Band take to the stage!"

The girls had been asked by their friends, the Music Fairies, to help them find their seven Magical Musical Instruments, which had been stolen from Fairyland's Royal School of Music by Jack Frost and his goblin servants. The Magical Musical Instruments were extremely important because they made music joyful and harmonious for everyone in both the human and fairy worlds. Since the instruments had gone missing, music everywhere had been ruined.

But Jack Frost had his own plans for the Magical Musical Instruments. Along with his goblin henchmen he had formed a pop group called Frosty and his Gobolicious Band, and he intended to use the magical powers of the instruments to win first prize in the National Talent Competition. Rachel and Kirsty had managed to return six of the Magical Musical Instruments to Fairyland, but they were still looking for Sadie's saxophone, and the girls knew that time was running out.

"I'm *so* worried that Jack Frost and the goblins are going to win the competition," Rachel confided to Kirsty

as they hurried towards the stage that had been set up at one end of the mall. "If Frosty and his Gobolicious Band win that recording contract with MegaBig Records, it won't be long before *everyone* finds out about the existence of Fairyland!"

"I know," Kirsty agreed. "And even though Jack Frost only has one of the Magical Musical Instruments left, its magic is so powerful that he'll probably win the competition anyway!"

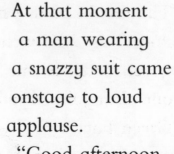

At that moment
a man wearing
a snazzy suit came
onstage to loud
applause.

"Good afternoon,
and welcome to the
first round of the
National Talent
Competition,"
the master
of ceremonies
announced. "We have some fantastic
acts for you to enjoy, and our judges
will select the best four. Those four will
then go forward to this afternoon's
LIVE, televised show!"

There were whoops of excitement
from the audience.

"The first band to perform are Green Factory," the MC went on. "So while they get ready, let me introduce you to our distinguished judges…"

"Green Factory!" Kirsty whispered excitedly to Rachel. "That sounds like a perfect name for a goblin band!"

"Yes, maybe Jack Frost has changed it from Frosty and his Gobolicious Band so we wouldn't recognise it," Rachel suggested. "Let's get a closer look at Green Factory, Kirsty!"

The girls tried to edge their way
closer to the stage, but there were so
many people around, they didn't get
very far. They had to stand on tiptoe
to look over the heads of the crowd
in front of them. Then they could
just catch the odd glimpse of Green
Factory at the side of the stage,
tuning up their instruments.

"They're all very short, Rachel,"
Kirsty pointed out. "*And* they're dressed
in green!"

Rachel nodded. The band were
wearing emerald-green trousers,
T-shirts and baseball caps.

"Remember that Jack Frost cast a
spell to make his goblins little-boy-sized
and flesh-coloured," Rachel whispered.
"Green Factory look *exactly* the right
size to be goblins!"

"I've spotted something else too!"
Kirsty gasped. She pointed to where the
stage lights were glinting on a shiny,
gold, musical instrument. "Rachel, they
have a saxophone!"

Green Factory

"So Green Factory *could* be Jack Frost's band!" Rachel exclaimed.

"Let's go backstage," Kirsty suggested. "We may be able to find Sadie's saxophone before Green Factory perform!"

The girls rushed backstage. There were lots of people milling about, so no one noticed Rachel and Kirsty slip into the wings.

"What now?" Rachel whispered.

Kirsty was staring closely at Green Factory. "Rachel, these aren't goblins!" she exclaimed. "The person with the saxophone is Courtney Lewis – she's a friend of mine from school!"

"Oh!" Rachel looked disappointed. "I really thought we'd found Sadie's saxophone!"

Just then, Courtney glanced over. She looked upset, but smiled as she spotted Kirsty.

"Hi, there," Courtney called. "What are you doing here, Kirsty?"

"We've come to wish you good luck," Kirsty replied, thinking fast. "This is my friend, Rachel."

"Hello." Courtney smiled at Rachel. "Meet the rest of Green Factory – Katie, Jess, Molly and Emma."

The girls grinned at Rachel and Kirsty.

"Are you nervous about performing today, Courtney?" Kirsty asked. "You looked a bit upset."

"Well, I've been practising really hard, but my saxophone sounds *awful*!" Courtney sighed. "I don't know what's wrong with it."

Rachel and Kirsty shared a secret glance. They knew exactly why Courtney's saxophone didn't sound right. It was because Jack Frost still had

the last Magical Musical Instrument!

"We're cutting my sax solo from our performance," Courtney went on. "I'm the lead singer, so I'll still get to perform, but we won't have a chance of winning if I play my saxophone. The audience will put their fingers in their ears!"

"And now for our first band," called

the MC. "It's the wonderful Green Factory!"

"Here we go!" Courtney held her saxophone out to Kirsty. "Would you look after this for me until we've finished our song?"

Kirsty nodded, taking the saxophone.

"Good luck!" she and Rachel chorused.

Courtney and the other girls hurried into the centre of the stage. Meanwhile, Rachel and Kirsty slipped out of the wings and rejoined the audience just as Green Factory launched into their song, *School Days*.

"This is great!" Rachel said enthusiastically to Kirsty after the first few bars.

"I never realised Courtney was so talented!" Kirsty replied.

"It's lucky the other six instruments are back in Fairyland," Rachel went on. "It means that music everywhere is almost back to normal now, and so Green Factory's talent can shine through!"

The song finished and the audience cheered loudly. Green Factory took a

bow and then hurried off into the
wings. Rachel was still applauding,
but Kirsty was staring down at
Courtney's saxophone, looking puzzled.

"Rachel!" Kirsty nudged her friend
as the MC announced the next band.
"Look at the saxophone!"

Rachel glanced down. To her
amazement, the shiny golden instrument
was jumping about in Kirsty's hands as
if it had a life of its own.

"It's like magic!" Rachel said, awestruck. "It *can't* be Sadie's saxophone because Courtney said it sounded awful, and the Magical Musical Instruments always play beautifully!"

Kirsty peered into the open end of the saxophone.

"Rachel, I can see glitter!" she whispered.

Rachel peeped in too, and saw a tiny burst of dazzling glitter deep inside the saxophone.

"It's me, girls," said a small voice.

"Sadie the Saxophone Fairy!"

Kirsty and Rachel grinned at each
other. Quickly they moved away from
the crowd and hid behind a display
of tall pot plants.

"You can come out now, Sadie!"
Rachel whispered.

Immediately, Sadie the Saxophone
Fairy burst out of the saxophone in
a mist of pale-blue sparkles!

Ice Rap

"Jack Frost is here at the competition, girls!" Sadie cried, floating down to land on Kirsty's shoulder. She wore a green and blue ruffled dress with a glittery cardigan around her shoulders, sparkly blue knee-length boots and a matching hairband. "We *have* to stop him from winning first prize. Everyone in Fairyland is relying on us!"

"We'll do our best, Sadie!" Rachel
assured her.

"I'd better give Courtney her
saxophone back, first," Kirsty said.

Sadie whizzed into Kirsty's pocket
and the girls hurried backstage to find
Courtney. She and
her band were
packing their
instruments away.

"Green Factory
were great,
Courtney!" Kirsty
said, handing over
the saxophone.

"You're bound to be in the final,"
Rachel added.

"Oh, I hope so!" Courtney replied.
"See you later."

"We'd better go and watch out for Frosty and his Gobolicious Band!" Kirsty whispered to Rachel as Green Factory went off to the dressing-room area.

The girls hurried back to join the audience. The band that had performed after Green Factory, a group of four teenage girls, were just finishing their song.

"We haven't seen any goblins yet, have we?" Rachel remarked. "There weren't even any backstage."

"They're probably hiding so we haven't got a chance of getting Sadie's saxophone back!" Kirsty replied.

The next entry was a rock group, and they were followed by six other bands, performing songs ranging from hip-hop to jazz. But there was no sign at all of Frosty and his Gobolicious Band. Sadie and the girls couldn't understand it.

"Where are Jack Frost and his goblins?" Sadie whispered, peeking over the top of Kirsty's pocket.

"Thank you, Red Socks!" the MC announced as the jazz band left the stage. "We're coming to the end of the show now, so if any other bands would like to take part, you'll have to be quick because the auditions will finish after the next act."

"This must be Jack Frost," Rachel murmured to Kirsty.

"Now for our final band before we find out which lucky four will go through to tonight's show," the MC said with a smile. "Please welcome – Mountain Snow!"

Rachel, Kirsty and Sadie watched eagerly, expecting to see Jack Frost and his goblins appear. But they were very surprised when a trio of rather elderly ladies walked out and began to yodel a pop song.

"They definitely aren't goblins!" Rachel whispered.

"Maybe Jack Frost decided not to enter the competition at all after losing the other six Magical Musical Instruments," Kirsty suggested.

"Then how will I ever find my saxophone?" Sadie sighed.

The yodelling song finished, and the crowd began to murmur in anticipation of hearing the result of the auditions. But suddenly the MC rushed onstage again.

"Ladies and gentlemen, we have a last-minute entry!" he shouted.

"I am pleased to introduce – Frosty and his Gobolicious Band!"

"So Jack Frost and his goblins *are* here!" Rachel gasped.

Jack Frost strutted onto the stage, waving at the audience. He was accompanied by a line of twelve grinning goblins.

"Look at the goblin at the end of the line!" Sadie said excitedly.

The girls saw that the last goblin was holding a golden saxophone. The saxophone was the only instrument onstage, and it seemed to give off a faint, magical shimmer.

"That's *mine!*" Sadie shouted, but her words were drowned out completely as Jack Frost picked up the microphone and the crowd broke into spontaneous applause.

"Hey, that lead singer's wearing such a cool costume!" said a young boy standing next to Rachel.

"Yeah, all those fake icicles look great!" his friend agreed.

"Listen up!" shouted Jack Frost as the saxophone goblin began to play.

*"I am Jack Frost
And you'd better know
That I am the king
Of ice and snow.
Don't mess with me
You'd better be nice,
Or I'll zap you with
My wand of ice!"*

Rachel, Kirsty and Sadie couldn't believe what they were hearing. The saxophonist goblin was playing his heart out, and his catchy tune, swooping from

high to low, somehow matched
perfectly with Jack Frost's rapping.
The goblins had divided into two
groups — one group was performing
backing vocals while the others were
clapping, whistling and snapping their
fingers in time to the music.

"Jack Frost and the goblins sound
amazing!" Rachel whispered to Kirsty.

The audience thought so too. When Jack Frost's rap finished, they burst into thunderous applause. Looking rather smug, Jack Frost and his goblins took a sweeping bow. Then they went off into the wings, Jack Frost waving graciously at the audience as he exited the stage.

"What are we going to do?" Sadie asked anxiously. "Frosty and his Gobolicious Band are bound to be one of the finalists if the audience's reaction is anything to go by!"

"Here's the MC to announce the results," said Kirsty.

The MC had been in consultation with the judges, but now he was back onstage again.

"I can now announce the four finalists for tonight's show!" he began, beaming broadly. "The first band to go through to the final is Green Factory!"

"Oh, good!" Kirsty exclaimed. "I'm so pleased for Courtney."

"And our next finalist—" The MC paused for a moment. "Frosty and his Goblicious Band!"

This time the audience clapped even more loudly. Rachel, Kirsty and Sadie stared at each other in deep dismay.

"Everyone loves Jack Frost and his goblins!" Rachel exclaimed. "They must be favourites to win the competition tonight!"

Sadie nodded. "And the only way we can stop him, girls," she said solemnly, "is to get my saxophone back before the finals take place!"

I'm a Celebrity!

Sadie ducked down out of sight into Kirsty's pocket again, and the girls immediately rushed backstage to find the goblin with the saxophone. But when they arrived, they were dismayed to find a large crowd of people clustered around Jack Frost, asking for his autograph.

"One at a time, please!" Jack Frost was saying loudly.

"Jack Frost is already acting like a star and he hasn't even won the competition yet!" Rachel murmured.

"There's Sadie's saxophone!" Kirsty whispered.

The saxophonist goblin was polishing the instrument with a cloth. As the girls watched, he put it away carefully into its case.

"Let's get a bit nearer to him," Rachel murmured. "But we must be careful. We don't want Jack Frost or the goblins to recognise us!"

The girls began edging their way towards the goblin with the saxophone.

"I must go to my dressing room and rest now," Jack Frost announced suddenly. "It's hard work being famous!"

He pointed to the tallest goblin.

"Keep an eye out for pesky girls or fairies!" Jack Frost ordered. "We can't risk losing the Magic Saxophone because we need it for the final."

The tall goblin nodded.

"Now let us be gone," Jack Frost snapped.

Immediately the other goblins cleared a path through the crowd and Jack Frost and the saxophone goblin swept through.

"Don't let them get away, girls!" Sadie whispered.

Rachel and Kirsty followed Jack Frost and the goblins towards the dressing rooms, but they had to keep their distance as the tall goblin kept looking round suspiciously.

"Fetch me some refreshments," Jack Frost demanded as they reached his dressing room. "Being a celebrity is hot and hungry work!" He grabbed the saxophone case from the goblin and marched inside, slamming the door behind him.

The girls watched as the goblins ran off to do Jack Frost's bidding. Meanwhile, the tallest goblin stationed himself outside the dressing room door.

"We have to find a way into that dressing room!" Kirsty whispered.

"But how are we going to get past the goblin bodyguard?" Rachel asked.

"Hello, are you girls part of the make-up team?" said a voice behind them.

Rachel and Kirsty turned and saw three teenage girls. They were carrying large wicker baskets full of beauty products.

"Er – yes," Rachel blurted out, glancing at Kirsty. This would be a perfect way to get into Jack Frost's dressing room!

"Oh, great," said one of the girls gratefully, handing Rachel a basket. "Any particular act you'd like to work with?"

"Frosty and his Gobolicious Band!" Kirsty and Rachel said eagerly.

The three girls laughed.

"You'd better get started then," one of the others remarked. "From the look of that band, it might take a while!"

"Good thinking, Rachel!" Sadie whispered, as the three girls went off. She fluttered out of Kirsty's pocket and dived quickly into the basket, hiding among the pots of make-up. "I'll try to grab my saxophone if I get the chance!"

Rachel and Kirsty hurried over to the bodyguard at the dressing room door.

"We're here to do Jack Frost's make-up," Kirsty explained.

The bodyguard stared at them suspiciously for a moment.

"OK," he scowled, opening the door. "But no funny business!"

Rachel and Kirsty went in. Jack Frost

was sitting at the dressing table, staring at his reflection in an illuminated mirror. The open saxophone case was on a table at the side of the room, the golden instrument glinting in the bright lights.

"What do *you* want?" Jack Frost snapped.

"We're here to do your make-up," Rachel said quickly.

"We'll make you look like a star!" Kirsty added.

Jack Frost smirked. "I like the sound of that!" he said.

Rachel put the basket of beauty products on the table next to the instrument case. Sadie peeped out and grinned as she saw her saxophone lying nearby.

"Let's start with your hair," Rachel said, grabbing a tube of hair gel.

She and Kirsty began applying gel to Jack Frost's icicles, making them stand up straight. Meanwhile, Jack Frost preened himself in the mirror.

Kirsty glanced over her shoulder. Sadie had sneaked silently out of the basket and was hovering above her saxophone.

But just then, the door burst open and the goblins charged in!

Shiny Saxophone

"It's not fair!" one of the goblins roared. "*I* want to play the saxophone next time!"

"No, it's my turn!" yelled another.

"SILENCE!" Jack Frost shouted.

The goblins shut up immediately.

"The goblin who played today is the ONLY one who's allowed to touch the saxophone," Jack Frost snapped. "Because he is the ONLY goblin who has managed to hang on to his Magical Musical Instrument!"

The other goblins hung their heads in shame. Meanwhile, Jack Frost turned to the saxophone-playing goblin.

"Make sure you polish the Magic Saxophone before the final tonight," he ordered loudly. "I want it to look nice and shiny!"

Kirsty and Rachel glanced at each other.

"It's lucky it's *us* here," Kirsty whispered. "What would the other make-up girls think, hearing Jack Frost talking about magic?"

"He obviously doesn't care a bit about keeping Fairyland secret!" Rachel replied.

One of the goblins rushed forwards to hand Jack Frost the drink he had requested, but his boss waved him away impatiently.

"I'm not hungry or thirsty any more," Jack Frost said airily. "I'm going to meet my public and sign more autographs!"

Jack Frost strutted out of the dressing room, his goblins scuttling after him. Only the saxophone player remained. He took the instrument out of the case and, sitting down at the dressing table, he began polishing it again.

"Any ideas, girls?" Sadie whispered as Kirsty and Rachel pretended to tidy the make-up basket. "Is there any way we can get my saxophone?"

"I don't think the goblin is going to put it down for a while," Rachel said under her breath. "He's polishing so hard, he'll make it disappear if he's not careful!"

Kirsty grinned. "That's given me an idea!" she exclaimed. "Sadie, could you magic up a polishing-cloth that will make the saxophone invisible? Then we might be able to grab it!"

"Sure thing!" Sadie agreed. She twirled her wand and a glittery pink cloth appeared in a cloud of fairy sparkles.

"You switch the cloths, Kirsty," Rachel

whispered, as Sadie jumped into Kirsty's pocket. "I'll distract the goblin by doing his make-up!"

The goblin was still polishing away, but he looked up suspiciously as Rachel went over to him.

"I'm here to do your make-up," she told him.

The goblin looked pleased. He put the cloth down, but kept hold of the saxophone.

Rachel opened a box of face powder and began to dab it onto the goblin's face with a large pad.

"Oh, that tickles!" the goblin laughed as he was surrounded by a cloud of white powder.

Meanwhile, Kirsty crept over, whisked away the polishing cloth and put the magic one in its place.

"Hey!" The goblin blinked at her through the mist of powder. "What are you doing?"

"I thought you might like a clean cloth," Kirsty said quickly. "Look, some powder has spilt onto your saxophone."

The goblin grabbed the magic cloth, laid the saxophone on his lap and began polishing. Kirsty, Rachel and Sadie watched eagerly.

"Jack Frost thinks he's the star of the band, but I'm the *real* star!" the goblin boasted.

Kirsty nudged Rachel as the open end of the saxophone began to disappear. But the goblin was too busy bragging to notice. Within seconds the entire instrument had vanished.

Suddenly the door flew open and Jack Frost and his goblins burst in.

"Why are you girls still here?" Jack Frost demanded furiously. "Get out! We need time to practise before tonight!" He glanced at the empty music case, then at the goblin sitting at the dressing table. "Where's the Magic Saxophone?"

The goblin looked down and his eyes almost popped out of his head.

"It was here a minute ago," he mumbled, jumping up.

"Ow!" Jack Frost roared. "Something just fell on my foot!"

"The invisible saxophone!" Rachel whispered to Kirsty, and the girls tried hard not to laugh.

As Jack Frost yelled at the goblin, Kirsty quietly bent down and felt around on the floor. Her hand closed over the invisible saxophone and she picked it up.

"Someone has stolen the saxophone!" Jack Frost yelled.

He glanced suspiciously at Rachel and Kirsty, but, of course, he couldn't see anything!

"Find the Magic Saxophone!" Jack Frost shouted at his goblins. "Or our performance in the final will be ruined!"

And they all dashed out of the

dressing room again.

Immediately Sadie zoomed over to the girls.

"Great work, you two!" she laughed, waving her wand over Kirsty's hand. The golden saxophone instantly appeared in a swirl of fairy dust, shrinking down to its Fairyland size.

"Thank you so much, girls—" Sadie began, clutching her saxophone tightly.

But all of a sudden an ice bolt whizzed straight past their heads.

Rachel, Kirsty and Sadie turned to see a furious Jack Frost standing in the doorway!

First Prize Goes to...

"Give me that saxophone!" Jack Frost shouted, preparing to launch another ice bolt.

Quickly, Sadie flicked her wand at Rachel and Kirsty. The magical sparkles surrounded the girls and instantly reduced them down to fairy-size. Then Sadie's magic whisked them straight off to Fairyland, just as another ice bolt flew across the room towards them.

"That was close!" Rachel gasped.

A few seconds later the three friends landed on the stage in the Fairyland Royal School of Music to cheers and applause. King Oberon, Queen Titania and the other six Music Fairies were waiting for them.

"You have the Magic Saxophone!"
Queen Titania said, beaming with
delight. "We knew you wouldn't let
us down, girls!"

"You have saved music everywhere!"
King Oberon announced. "And now we
shall have a wonderful music show to
celebrate the return of the Magical
Musical Instruments.
Thank you, girls!"

He stepped
forwards and
handed two small
golden boxes to
Rachel and
Kirsty. The
boxes shimmered
very slightly with
fairy magic.

"They are magical music players," the King explained with a smile. "They will play all your favourite fairy music whenever you like!"

Rachel and Kirsty beamed at each other.

"Thank you!" they cried.

"And will you stay for our musical celebration?" Queen Titania invited them.

"Thank you, but I think we'd better go back and watch the final of the competition," Rachel replied.

"What about Jack Frost?" Kirsty asked anxiously. "Do you think his band might still win tonight, even without the Magical Instruments?"

"Don't worry," Queen Titania laughed. "Without the Magical Musical

Instruments, the true standard of Jack
Frost's musical ability will be revealed!"

"Goodbye!" the girls called as the
queen lifted her wand to send them
back home.

"Goodbye, and thank you!"
the Music Fairies chorused.

Rachel and Kirsty felt
themselves whizzed away
in a whirl of magic,
sweet fairy music
tinkling in their
ears. A few
seconds later
they were back
in the mall and
were normal
girls once
more.

"Please welcome back the fantastic Green Factory!" the MC was saying.

"Look!" Kirsty nudged Rachel as Green Factory's song began. "Courtney's got her saxophone!"

The girls were thrilled to see that Green Factory performed even more brilliantly than they had done before. Courtney's saxophone solo sounded perfect, too.

"That's because Sadie's saxophone is back in Fairyland!" Rachel said, as they joined in the deafening applause.

"And now our next performance is by Frosty and his Gobolicious Band!" announced the MC.

Jack Frost and his goblins hurried on stage. As Green Factory passed by, Jack Frost snatched the saxophone from

Courtney's hand and passed it to the
goblin who had played earlier. Then
Jack Frost grabbed the microphone and
began his rap.

"*I am Jack Frost...* he sang.

But unlike before, his voice
sounded harsh and
cracked.

Meanwhile,
the goblin with
the saxophone
was trying to
play it, but
merely succeeded
in producing strange
honking sounds. Behind
them, the other goblins were
trying to sing, clap and whistle,
but it sounded terrible.

69

"They've got no rhythm at all without the Magic Saxophone!" Rachel laughed, as the audience glanced at each other in confusion.

"You're doing it all wrong!" one of the goblins yelled, pulling his neighbour's nose.

"No, you are!" shrieked the other goblin.

Within minutes the goblins were arguing and wrestling each other around the stage. The MC immediately rushed on, looking very flustered.

"And a big thank you to Frosty and his Gobolicious Band for their – er – unique performance!" he mumbled.

"I haven't finished yet!" Jack Frost snarled, glaring at him.

Two security guards ran out from the wings and escorted Jack Frost, complaining loudly, from the stage. The goblins hurried off too, still arguing.

"I don't think Frosty and his Gobolicious Band are going to win!" Kirsty laughed.

The girls watched the other two acts and then waited impatiently for the MC to announce the results.

"And the first prize of a recording contract with MegaBig Records goes to…" There was a loud drum roll. "GREEN FACTORY!"

"Well done, Courtney!" Kirsty cried, as Green Factory returned to the stage to collect their recording contract from the president of MegaBig Records.

"Rachel, isn't it brilliant?"

Rachel nodded. "Green Factory really deserve to win," she replied. "And I'm so glad that music everywhere is back to normal again!"

"Me too," Kirsty agreed. "The world would be very dull without music, wouldn't it?"

"And very dull without our fairy friends, too!" Rachel winked at Kirsty. "I wonder what our next fairy adventure will be?"

Now Rachel and Kirsty have helped
the Music Fairies, it's time to help

Gabriella
the Snow Kingdom Fairy

Each year, Gabriella the Snow
Kingdom Fairy makes the festive
season a happy and peaceful time.
But when her magical objects go
missing, everything starts to go wrong!
Kirsty and Rachel must help her find
them so everyone can enjoy happy
holidays once again...

A Fairy Snowball!

"We're going to try out the snow," Kirsty Tate called to her mum. "We'll be back for lunch, OK?"

"See you later!" Rachel Walker shouted to her mum and dad.

The two friends grinned at each other as their parents called back goodbyes.

Both girls were wearing new salopettes, puffa jackets, woolly hats and gloves. Kirsty pushed open the door of the chalet, and out they stepped, blinking in the bright sunshine.

Mountain peaks rose majestically all around, covered in thick white snow. Skiers were already whizzing down the slopes, zig-zagging across the mountainside like colourful dots. Other people were careering about on snowboards, sun glinting off their snow goggles.

Rachel couldn't stop smiling. "It's so fantastic, being on holiday with you again!" she said happily.

Kirsty nodded. "I know," she said, linking arms with her best friend. "All this snow, and the Winter Festival in a few days to look forward to, as well." She beamed. "And you never know, we might meet a fairy too. We always have such magical adventures when we're together!"

The girls' parents had rented them skis and a snowboard each, and Rachel and Kirsty went to find them in the small shed at the side of the chalet. "I'm going to try my skis first," Kirsty decided, taking a pair of ski poles, skis and special ski-boots. She sat down to put them on, feeling tingly with excitement.

"I'll try a snowboard," Rachel said eagerly, picking up a turquoise board that was long and slender, with rounded ends.

Once they were both ready, they found a small slope to practise on.

"Wheeee!" Kirsty squealed, pushing off. "Here I go!" She whizzed down the slope, but wobbled at the end and fell sideways into the snow. Ouch! It was hard and icy. She got to her feet gingerly, rubbing her legs.

"My turn now... Wheeee!" cried Rachel, standing on her board and riding downhill on it. It was hard keeping her balance, though, and she fell off too. "Ow!" she cried, as her elbow bumped on a particularly hard patch of ice. "This snow isn't very soft, is it...?"

Read the rest of

Gabriella
the Snow Kingdom Fairy

to find out what magic happens next...

(available now!)

The Music Fairies

Win Rainbow Magic goodies!

In every book in the Rainbow Magic Music Fairies series (books 64-70) there is a hidden picture of a musical note with a secret letter in it. Find all seven letters and rearrange them to make a special Music Fairies word, then send it to us. Each month we will put the entries into a draw and select one winner to receive a Rainbow Magic Sparkly T-shirt and Goody Bag!

Send your entry on a postcard to Rainbow Magic Music Fairies Competition, Orchard Books, 338 Euston Road, London NW1 3BH. Australian readers should write to Hachette Children's Books, Level 17/207 Kent Street, Sydney, NSW 2000.
New Zealand readers should write to Rainbow Magic Competition, 4 Whetu Place, Mairangi Bay, Auckland, NZ. Don't forget to include your name and address. Only one entry per child.
Final draw: 30th September 2009.

Good luck!

Have you checked out the

website at:
www.rainbowmagic.co.uk

Look out for the Magical Animal Fairies!

ASHLEY
THE DRAGON FAIRY
978-1-40830-349-8

LARA
THE BLACK CAT FAIRY
978-1-40830-350-4

ERIN
THE FIREBIRD FAIRY
978-1-40830-351-1

RIHANNA
THE SEAHORSE FAIRY
978-1-40830-352-8

SOPHIA
THE SNOW SWAN FAIRY
978-1-40830-353-5

LEONA
THE UNICORN FAIRY
978-1-40830-354-2

CAITLIN
THE ICE BEAR FAIRY
978-1-40830-355-9

Available April 2009